Special thanks:

Jensen, India, and Martin Schmitt; Britta Bushnell
and the Kessel Family; Jill and Dylan Williams;
Sean Cramer; Nora Cohen; Melissa Hertz;
Lisa Misraje Bentley; The Topanga Playgroup;
John Feldsted; the Ganz Family; Star Oakland;
Craig Goldberg; Tiffany (Chicken) Siegel; and
Ewgene (Bobby Hailstorm) Ewing.

©2007 Sue Ganz-Schmitt

All Rights Reserved

No part of this publication may be reproduced, stored
in a retrieval system, or transmitted in any form or by
any means, electronic or mechanical (including
photocopying and recording), without the permission
of the author.

First published by:

Wild Indigo Publishing
Topanga, CA 90290
310-455-2400

And:

Dog Ear Publishing
4010 W. 86th Street, Suite H
Indianapolis, IN 46268
www.dogearpublishing.net

ISBN: 978-159858-302-1
Library of Congress Control Number: 2011928330
Printed in the United States of America

The information in this book is intended to provide
helpful and informative material on the subject
addressed. It is not intended to replace professional
medical advice. Any use of the information in this
book is at the reader's discretion. The author and
publisher specifically disclaim any and all liability
arising directly or indirectly from the use or
application of any information contained in the book.
A health care professional should be consulted
regarding your specific situation.

This book is a fictional work. Please do not attempt the
acts described herein at home.

EVEN SUPERHEROES GET DIABETES

by Sue Ganz-Schmitt

Illustrated by
Micah Chambers-Goldberg

You are a child of the universe,
no less than the trees and stars.
-Max Ehrmann

Hi. My name's Super K, but my friends call me Kelvin. I was an expert on superheroes, even before I became one.

At kindergarten, I saved the day from pirates, sharks, hot lava, and all the bad guys you can think of.

But back then, I was just pretending.

Every day, after school, my little brother and I saved the neighborhood until dark, when Mom called, "Time for your hero sandwiches!"

At bedtime, Dad read me a stack of books about superheroes. My favorites were Ratman, Slimegirl, and KiteBoy.

"Dad, how do you get superpowers?" I always asked.

Dad had lots of theories, but I could tell he didn't really know.

That's because no one in the universe knows how superheroes are chosen to have superpowers.

What I do know is that it always starts with a bad day. That's how it was with me.

I don't know why I was chosen to become a superhero... I just was.

When my bad day started, I had been waiting three forevers for KiteBoy's new movie:

"KiteBoy vs. the Scissoring Samurai."

The big day was finally here.

Dad was out jogging. After that, he was going to take me to the matinee.

"Waffles with strawberries and whipped cream!" sang Mom that morning.

I was starving! But I couldn't move, even for my favorite breakfast.

Had VacuumHead snuck into my room and sucked out all my energy?

We were in a room as big as an airplane hangar. Machines were buzzing, flashing, and beeping. It was better than a NASA space center.

The doctor hooked me up to these electrodes with long wires. "Jump!" he commanded.

I bounced high, like on a trampoline. I felt strange, like when I was rock jumping earlier.

"It's just as I thought!" he said, smiling.

I glanced at the doctor and noticed his extra-muscly arms. My eyes spotted something lumpy under his coat that bulged around his side. What was that thing?

"I need you to put on this anti-gravity suit," he said. He gave me more tests. I was like an astronaut in training.

"Don't worry, sir. We'll take care of it!" I said.

The Captain winked at me, and we took off.

We reached Chloe just before snack time.

"Light speed!" yelled the Captain, and we were off to another mission.

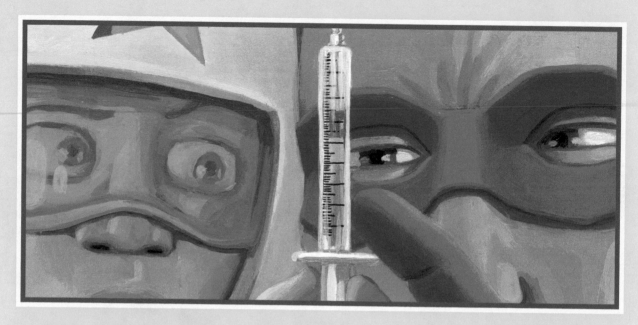

On most missions, we had to bring insulin to kids, but once in a while, we had to help parents read the tiny lines on the injection syringe.

Other times, we had to fly a case of insulin to a hospital that had run out—like in Tibet, Guatemala, and Zimbabwe.

We flew anywhere there were diabetic kids, which, as the Captain explained to me, is everywhere!

One day, after school, Mom and my brother ran over to me. "Here," said Mom, handing me my superhero clothes.

"Captain Fly-A-Betes called," she said. "He needs you to meet him at his office right away for a mission."

Now, there were some kids at school who already thought my **super-pump-pack** was the coolest thing they had ever seen. But you should have seen their faces when I did the old up, up, and away!

That night, at bedtime, I had to explain something to Dad that he was always wondering about.

"Dad, it doesn't really matter how you get superpowers... the thing that matters is—how you use 'em."

**Dedicated to Kaden Kessel (K.K.),
a real diabetes superhero.**

TYPE 1 DIABETES
How it works:

1. You eat some food or drink some juice.

2. The juice drops break apart inside your body and turn into sugar.

3. Sugar is the same thing as glucose.

4. Glucose goes into your blood.

5. Your pancreas is like a machine that makes stuff called "insulin."

6. Insulin goes into your blood and makes friends with glucose.

7. Insulin carries glucose to the rest of your body.

8. **TYPE 1 DIABETES is** when your pancreas doesn't make the insulin you need, so you need to take insulin medicine.

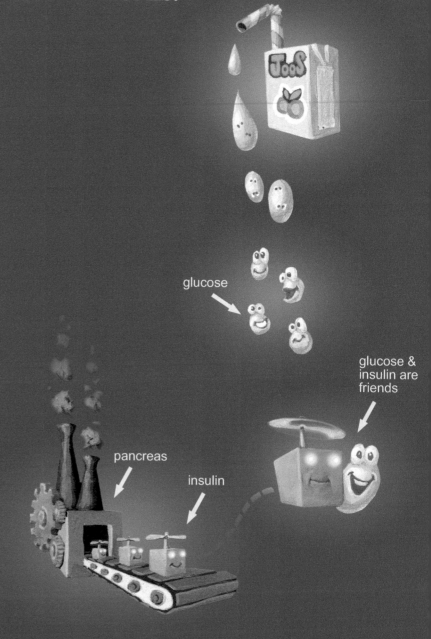

glucose

glucose & insulin are friends

pancreas

insulin

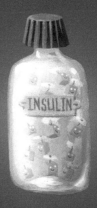

SUPER K's DIABETES DECODER

Autoimmune Disease – When we get sick, our bodies fight the germs and viruses, so we stay healthy. Some people's bodies get confused. Instead of just fighting the germs and viruses, their bodies attack some of their healthy parts. Type 1 diabetes is a kind of autoimmune disease.

Blood Sugar – This is sugar that's in our blood. It's important that the amount doesn't get too high or too low. Blood sugar is also called "glucose."

Carbohydrates – These are some foods that are carbohydrates: bread, noodles, juice, sugar, honey, and syrup. Our bodies turn carbohydrates into energy.

Diabetes (Type 1) – This is when the body gets confused and attacks the cells that make insulin in the pancreas. Then there isn't enough insulin to help the blood sugar turn into energy. Too much sugar stays in the blood. If you have type 1 diabetes, you MUST take insulin.

Diabetes (Type 2) – This is when the body CAN make insulin. But either it doesn't make enough, or the body doesn't use it the right way. Some people with type 2 diabetes need insulin, but not everyone. Only people with type 2 diabetes can help control their diabetes with medicine that is swallowed. Eating healthy food and exercising also helps to control their diabetes.

Diabetes Symptoms – These are clues that someone has diabetes. Some people feel like they have the flu, they have to pee a lot, or they might be really thirsty. They may be really hungry and tired, too. Their breath might smell like fruit.

Glucose Test Kit – This kit helps people keep track of their blood sugar. It has a finger prick to get out some drops of blood. Then the blood goes on a test strip. The test strip goes into a meter that measures the sugar in the blood.

Honeymoon Period – This is when a person first gets diabetes and doesn't need very much insulin because his or her blood sugar is almost normal again.

Insulin – This helps blood sugar get out of the blood and into the cells. Then the cells can turn it into energy for the body.

Insulin Injections – People who don't make insulin need to get the insulin into their bodies. Some people get insulin shots. These are also called "injections."

Insulin Pump – This is a mini-computer that diabetic people can wear. It puts insulin into their bodies when they need it. It's another way to get insulin.

Pancreas – This is the part of the body that makes insulin. The pancreas is behind the stomach and is about as big as a hand.

CPSIA information can be obtained
at www.ICGtesting.com
Printed in the USA
LVHW070533270819
629069LV00012B/170/P